DOG SHOW

ELIZABETH WINTHROP

ILLUSTRATED BY
MARK ULRIKSEN

HENRY HOLT AND COMPANY · NEW YORK

Every year in May, the town of Bonesport put on a dog show. The mayor and the police chief and the fire chief were the judges. There were classes for black dogs and brown dogs, long-haired dogs and short-haired dogs, dogs with spots and dogs with droopy ears. There were classes for dogs in costumes and dogs who did tricks and dogs who stood very still and dogs who couldn't stand still for one single minute.

When Harvey heard about the dog show, he was very excited. Fred was not. Harvey planned for months. Fred hoped the day would never come.

One day Harvey came home from the store with a great big bag. Fred poked his nose inside and sniffed. It didn't smell like bone crunchies or his favorite liver treats.

"Fred," said Harvey, "I'm making our costumes. I will play the lion, and you will play the tamer. Won't that surprise them?"

Fred pushed his dog bowl around the kitchen floor, but Harvey didn't get the hint. He was too busy cutting and sewing.

The day of the dog show Harvey got up early. He and Fred tried on their costumes. Fred wore a red jacket with gold buttons. Harvey wore a lion suit with a silky mane and big floppy paws. Fred thought Harvey looked silly in his lion costume. The mane kept getting tangled in his teeth. But Fred loved Harvey. He didn't want to hurt his feelings.

Harvey combed Fred's hair and cleaned his ears.
He tried to brush Fred's teeth, but Fred clamped
his jaws together and shook his head. No matter
how much Fred loved Harvey, he didn't let anybody
brush his teeth.

Harvey gave Fred a big breakfast with an extra
liver treat. Harvey practiced his roaring in between
bites of scrambled egg. Fred thought he sounded
pretty silly, but he barked every now and then just
to make Harvey feel good.

The whole town turned out for the dog
show. Dogs that Fred hadn't seen in years
barked a greeting.

The police chief blew his whistle.
"Dogs can be entered in as many classes
as they wish," announced the fire chief.
The mayor called for all the black dogs
to come into the ring.

The six black dogs walked in a circle around the judges. The judges whispered to each other. The dogs sniffed each other. The owners waited nervously.

"The blue ribbon goes to Muffin the Labrador, the blackest dog in this circle," said the police chief.

Muffin's owner jumped up and down.

"One more lap around the ring," the mayor said. "Ladies and gentlemen, a round of applause for the BLACK DOGS."

People clapped. Dogs yapped. Flags snapped in the wind. Fred yawned.

It was going to be a long day.

Harvey entered Fred in every class he could. They competed in SPOTTED DOGS, but Fred had more splotches than spots.

They entered the class for DOGS WHO STAND VERY STILL, but Fred got a terrible itch on his back leg just as the judges were looking at him.

They walked into the ring for DOGS WITH DROOPY EARS, but the judges gave the prize to Larry the coonhound, whose ears hung all the way down to the ground.

They didn't win in SHORT DOGS or SHORT-HAIRED DOGS or DOGS WHO CAN'T STAND STILL, because Fred was simply too tired by that time to move one bone in his body.

"Wait till they see our lion show," Harvey whispered to Fred. "We're bound to win first place in that one."

Fred wasn't so sure. It was hot. His tongue was hanging out.

Finally, DOGS IN COSTUMES was announced. Harvey bounded into the ring. He roared. Fred stood on his hind legs and barked. Harvey batted a floppy paw at Fred. Fred barked again.

The judges whispered. First prize went to Daisy the dachshund, who was dressed as a pea pod. Fred and Harvey won an honorable mention.

Harvey trudged out of the ring, his tail
dragging on the ground. Fred licked his hand,
but Harvey didn't even notice.

"Come on, Fred," Harvey said. "It's time
to go home." He gave Fred a liver treat and
hooked up his leash.

But Fred dug in his back paws and refused
to budge.

"Heel, Fred," said Harvey.

But Fred would not heel. He barked at Harvey and yanked on the leash. He dragged Harvey right across the ring and up to the judges' table. There he stood, his head held high.

The judges whispered together. Finally the mayor put up her hand for silence.

"Ladies and gentlemen, in the last competition of the day, Dogs Who Look Like Their Owners, first prize goes to . . .

. . . Fred the basset hound and his look-alike owner, Harvey! Let's give them a big hand."

The crowd whooped and cheered and stomped their feet.

With his chin lifted and his ears flapping, Fred led Harvey around the ring. The judges pinned one blue ribbon on Harvey's chest and another on Fred's collar.

Harvey beamed. Fred barked.

The crowd clapped. Flags flapped. Puppies yapped.

And now, Fred said to himself, it's time to go home.